Mama Rex & T

The Prize

by Rachel Vail

illustrations by Steve Björkman

ORCHARD BOOKS
An Imprint of Scholastic Inc.
New York

To Magda, with love and gratitude.

—RV

For Andrew Whitt.

—SB

Library of Congress-in-Publication Data available.
ISBN 0-439-47191-5

10 9 8 7 6 5 4 3 2   03 04 05 06 07

Book design by Elizabeth Parisi

Printed in the U.S.A.
First Scholastic edition, February 2003

Contents

"**P**lease," begged T.

"Oh, T," said Mama Rex. "It's a waste of money."

T looked sadly at the machines lined up near the entrance to the supermarket. Inside one there were some great gobs of goo. Another had huge rainbow gumballs. In the last machine, T saw something really awesome: glow-in-the-dark skeleton guys.

"It's not a waste to me," said T. "To me, this stuff is treasure."

"Come on, T," said Mama Rex, pulling him by the sleeve. "We're in a hurry."

"We're always in a hurry," grumbled T. "I hate shopping."

Mama Rex sighed and knelt in front of T.

"The bake sale at school is tomorrow," she explained. "I signed up to make a fruit tart. You know what's in the fruit bin right now?"

T shook his head.

"Nail polish."

T tried not to smile.

"I don't think Nail Polish Tart will sell very well," said Mama Rex. "Do you?"

T shrugged. "Why can't we just buy a box of doughnuts again?" suggested T.

"That was so humiliating last year," groaned Mama Rex. "All the other parents had baked beautiful masterpieces...."

"So?" asked T.

"So," said Mama Rex, "this year I'm not bringing supermarket doughnuts. I'm baking, from scratch, a cranberry-currant conserve tart."

"Yuck," said T. "What's that?"

"I don't know," said Mama Rex. "Come on, let's just get the ingredients. OK?"

"OK," said T. "Nail polish is not a fruit."

"Exactly! Tell you what..."

"What?" asked T.

Mama Rex stepped on a black mat. The automatic door slid open. T followed Mama Rex into the supermarket.

"If you can be very helpful in here..." began Mama Rex, yanking on a shopping cart.

"Yeah?" T asked hopefully.

"And don't whine or cause any trouble at all..." Mama Rex yanked harder on the cart. It still didn't budge from the smoosh of carts.

"Yeah?" asked T again, imagining himself playing all afternoon with a glow-in the-dark skeleton guy.

"Then I — ugh!" grunted Mama Rex as she tugged with all her might. The cart ripped away from the others. Mama Rex sailed backward, past T, and landed on her tail. T rushed over and helped her up.

"Oof," said Mama Rex.

"You were saying?" T prompted her.

"I was saying," said Mama Rex, "that if you can be a real help getting the groceries, I think you'll deserve some kind of prize at the end."

T smiled. "The kind of prize that, when you
put quarters in the machine and turn the knob,
it tumbles down?"
Mama Rex nodded.
"A glow-in-the-dark-skeleton-guy kind of prize?"
Mama Rex nodded.
"Hooray!" said T. "Let's get groceries!"

Chapter 2
GROCERY PROBLEMS

Mama Rex pulled a long list out of her pocketbook.

"Wow," said T. "All that?"

Mama Rex nodded.

"Maybe we could just make popcorn," suggested T.

"T..." said Mama Rex, in a warning voice.

"Just kidding," said T. "What do we need first?"

"A thin-skinned orange," said Mama Rex.

"Thin-skinned?" asked T. "Why? And how do you tell?"

"I have no idea." Mama Rex scratched her head. "We also need fresh cranberries and dried currants."

"Let's try the fruit area," suggested T.

He ran up the aisle, ahead of Mama Rex.

He wanted to be helpful. He wanted to be fast.

But first he wanted to stop at the bakery counter.

"Uh, T?" said Mama Rex when she caught up.

"I know," whispered T, waiting nicely to be noticed. "Just a sec."

"Well, hello, T," said the lady behind the counter. "You're looking sharp today."

"Thank you," answered T.

"Always so polite," said the bakery lady. "May I offer you a cookie?"

T smiled. He looked up at Mama Rex.

"OK," said Mama Rex.

"Hooray!" T pointed at the cookie with the most rainbow sprinkles.

"I was saving that one just for you," said the bakery lady.

She chose a piece of waxed paper from a box. T watched through the glass as she lifted his cookie from the display. He couldn't help jumping a little as the bakery lady came around the counter and handed him the cookie.

"Thank you!" shouted T.

"You're very welcome," said the bakery lady. Then she turned to Mama Rex and said, "What a nice young dinosaur you have there."

"He's the best," said Mama Rex, following T down the next aisle.

As T walked along, munching on his cookie, he passed a baby in a cart. The baby was screaming "Mine! Mine!" and grabbing things off the shelves. His drooping mother was screaming "No! No!" and putting the things back.

"Can I sit in the cart?" T asked Mama Rex.

"You're too big," said Mama Rex.

T tried to climb in, but Mama Rex was right.

Behind them, the baby grabbed a jar of applesauce and threw it.

SMASH!

"Mess," said the baby, pointing at the floor.

"Did I do that when I was a baby?" whispered T.

Mama Rex nodded, maneuvering the cart around the glunk of applesauce.

"Good thing I'm big now, huh?" asked T. "And helpful. Oops!" T clamped his hand over his mouth to keep the cookie crumbs in.

He had forgotten about the ingredients — and
the prize! T put his half-eaten cookie on the seat
of the cart. "I'm done," he said and sprinted
around the corner.

T glanced up the next aisle.

Cereal and peanut butter.

He kept going.

He passed the aisle of cans and then the toilet
paper aisle. He paused at the candy aisle, but
only for a second. He turned down the toothpaste
aisle, but there was nothing new or improved.

He came to the fruit area. "I found it," yelled T. "That was helpful, right?"

"Yes," said Mama Rex. "Can you help me find a thin-skinned orange?"

T nodded.

He passed the apples. He passed the berries.

He almost passed the grapes, but stopped for a sample.

He passed the lemons and limes.

He found the oranges.

There were navel oranges, juice oranges, organic oranges, and blood oranges. "Don't get blood oranges," said T nervously.

He pulled a nice-looking orange from the bottom of the juice orange pile. An orange from the top tumbled down.

T caught it.

Another orange chased the first one down.

And another.

And another.

T tried to catch the avalanche of oranges. He caught some in his arms, but then a falling grapefruit bonked him on the nose, which tipped him off balance so much that his tail clonked the honeydews.

T had become fruit salad.

Mama Rex found his arm and pulled him out from under the fruit. T had one orange in each hand and a frown on his face.

"I think those are thin-skinned oranges!"
exclaimed Mama Rex.

"Yeah?" asked T.

Mama Rex placed them into the cart and said
"We're sorry" to the guys who were picking up all
the fruit from the floor.

"Happens every day," said the small guy.

"Could you point me toward the dried
currants?" she asked.

"Aisle seven," said the big guy.

T pushed the cart behind Mama Rex as she chose the rest of the ingredients on her list. He sadly unloaded the things from the cart onto the check-out belt.

He thought about how much fun he would've had with a glow-in-the-dark skeleton guy, if only he'd been able to be helpful.

Chapter 3
THE PRIZE

T followed Mama Rex out the sliding door. He was looking down at his feet, so he didn't notice that Mama Rex had stopped until he slammed into her back.

"Oof," said T.

"Maybe after we get your prize," said Mama Rex, "we should go back in and buy some doughnuts, just in case the fruit tart turns out disgusting."

"What did you say?" asked T.

"Doughnuts. I never actually baked a tart before, so what if it's gross?"

"Before that," said T.

Mama Rex put down her bags and held out her fist. T tapped it.

Mama Rex turned her hand over and opened her fingers. T saw two quarters in her palm.

"But I made a mess," said T.

"You sure did." Mama Rex laughed. "But you were also very helpful."

"I guess I was." T straightened up. "We don't need doughnuts. We'll make the best fruit tart ever."

He took the two quarters, wedged them into the slot, and turned the knob.

Ka-junk!

T opened the little door and caught the plastic bubble. He yanked and tugged and tore until the two halves split apart. A small plastic skeleton guy fell on the floor.

T scooped him up.

"You like him?" asked Mama Rex.

"I love him!" shouted T. He held the skeleton guy up for Mama Rex to see. A leg fell off.

"Hmm," said T. "Well, that's easy to fix."

"Good," said Mama Rex.

T picked up the leg and worked it back into the hip socket. "See?"

Then the head dropped off.

"Hey," said T. "Well, that's no problem, you just have to..."

T stuck out his tongue, concentrating. He screwed the head back on.

"There!"

Both arms popped off. Mama Rex bent down
and picked up the arms. She took the skeleton
guy gently from T.

"Maybe I can fix it," she told him.

Mama Rex jiggled an arm into its socket.

Both legs plopped out.

The ribs crumpled.

Then the head went zinging off and smacked Mama Rex in the eye.

"I'm not having a lot of luck," admitted Mama Rex.

"Neither is the skeleton guy," said T.

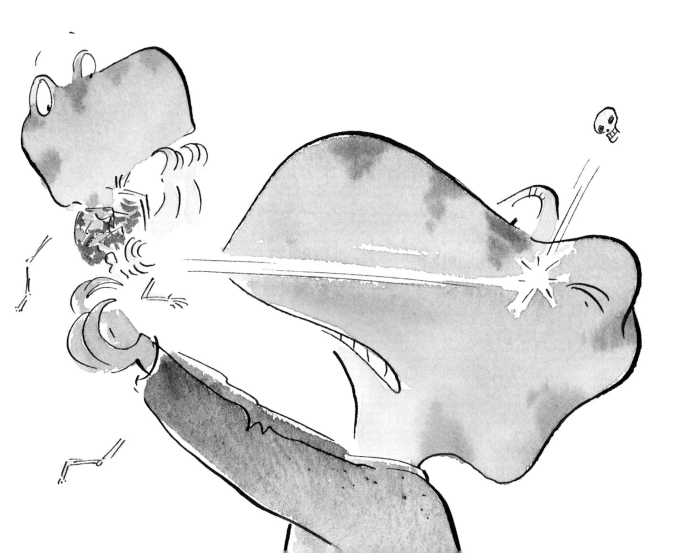

T watched as a kid and her mom were going into the supermarket. The girl shrieked, "Can I get one of those glow-in-the-dark skeleton guys?"

"Maybe on the way out," said the mom.

"Should we warn them?" asked Mama Rex.

T shook his head. "It won't work."

"It might still glow," said T. "But, anyway, a bunch of bones in a bubble...that's a pretty good prize for making a mess in the supermarket. Right?"

They walked down the street together.

Mama Rex smiled at T. "You're my prize," she said to him.

He gathered the pieces from all over the floor and placed them into the plastic bubble, which he jammed shut.

"I'm sorry," said Mama Rex. "You deserve a good prize."